SQUASH BALLS

Also by Barry Waters

Piste Again
Back on the Piste
The Tennis Racket
Wish We Weren't Here: A Survival Guide to Abroad

SQUASH BALLS

A SURVIVAL GUIDE TO THE GAME

BARRY WATERS Illustrated by Graham Thompson

Roger Houghton
London

First published 1986

Set in Korinna by Gee Graphics Ltd

Printed and bound in Great Britain by Mackays of Chatham Ltd
for Roger Houghton Ltd, in association with J. M. Dent and Sons Ltd,
Aldine House, 33 Welbeck Street, London W1M 8LX

British Library Cataloguing in Publication Data
Waters, Barry
Squash balls: a survival guide to the game.
1. Squash rackets (Game)——Anecdotes, facetiae, satire, etc.
I. Title
796.34'3'0207 GV1004

ISBN 1 85203 003 8

Contents

Introduction

'Alas, regardless of their doom,
The little victims play!'

Thomas Gray, 'Ode on a Distant Prospect of Eton College'

Not so long ago, squash, to most people, simply meant something you drank on a hot summer's day. We now know different. No one today can fail to be familiar with this peculiar form of self-destruction, masquerading as a sport, where two adults scurry around in a big white box, like rats in a trap, swinging wildly at each other, and at the same time trying to put to death a little black ball bouncing around on the blood-spattered walls.

Why ever do they do it? You may well ask. It's a question that squash addicts all over the world put to themselves every day as, with trembling hands and frog in throat, they pick up the phone to arrange their next league match.

Surely there are easier ways of deciding who should pay for the drinks, or, for that matter, of committing suicide. Probably. But no one seems to have told them. They still keep at it, charging around that windowless torture chamber, frothing at the mouth, totally absorbed in their ritual of mutual flagellation. And, what's more, they're doing it in *ever-increasing numbers*. The Squash Rackets Association claim that there are more than 3 million players in Britain alone (though that, of course, may mean that there are more than 3 million Britons who *claim* to play).

Now you might think that squash is merely an eccentric Anglo-Saxon aberration. But you'd be wrong. It seems there is no shortage of devout sado-masochists in countries like Finland, Germany, Japan and Switzerland. There, too, they are also fast discovering the dubious delights of this licensed form of assault and battery, which, according to its promoters, is now the world's fastest-growing game. It's a trend which Britain and the other traditional squash-playing nations like Australia, Canada, South Africa, and those former outposts of the Empire like Egypt and Pakistan, are doing their best to encourage – constantly sending forth missionaries like the venerable 'Monk' Barrington to spread ever wider their gospel of Grievous Bodily Harm.

The reason why there are so many converts remains a mystery. Perhaps squash is, as the promoters say, 'the game of our times' – a fast year-round all-weather 'instant' exercise potion, the effects of which, in a mere half hour, can be felt in parts of your body which other games cannot begin to reach. Perhaps it's the novelty; squash is played, for the most part, in clubs and 'leisure' centres, with sauna baths and all the other latest facilities – like Space Invaders and slot machines – in the lounge bar. (The world's newest class of millionaires are the squash court manufacturers and racket club entrepreneurs.)

One thing, however, is for sure. Even if it's *not* your game, squash is unavoidable. If your tennis club, or cricket club or rugby club doesn't have squash courts attached, it soon will. Increasingly, it's all those tokens dropped in squash court light-meters over the winter months which keep tennis and cricket clubs in business. Who knows, there may even come a day when it becomes the Wimbledon All England *Squash Rackets*, Lawn Tennis and Croquet Club. Well, maybe.

The fact that everyone else seems to be doing it, of course, is no reason why you too should turn yourself into a purple-faced racket-flailing zombie. People like Jonah may well be having a whale of a time chasing down that 100 m.p.h. ball, as they crash through new pain barriers. But that doesn't necessarily mean it's a good idea for the rest of us to chase cardiac arrest or cerebral concussion, as we crash through the walls.

Nevertheless, it has to be said – and this may come as something of a surprise – that there are *some* things to be said for the game. Squash-players, for instance, do enjoy a certain respect. The physical rigours involved mean that if you mention to a non-player that squash is your game, you'll probably be treated at the very least as a black belt fourth dan. And even though it's now a game for the masses, squash has not yet entirely lived down its 'posh' public school origins; despite all those Space Invader machines, it still has a certain cachet. There are 'social' benefits too – some clubs could almost pass as singles bars if they didn't have those damned courts attached. Then there's the business side: now that every other hard-charging executive has a squash racket sticking out of his briefcase, more and more deals seem to be concluded on the squash court. (A talent for losing graciously can prove invaluable on these occasions). The sad fact is, of course, that in today's 'leisured' unemployment society most of us do feel required to take up at least one racket game (regardless of whether we can afford it or not), and squash is one of the options.

The principal *dis*advantage is that (unlike some other racket games, such as tennis) squash prides itself on being a *participant* rather than spectator sport. It's true that they can now rig up 'fish bowls' at places like the Albert Hall, so that thousands of enthusiasts can watch other people suffering; you even get squash on telly from time to time; and the trend in clubs is towards bigger galleries, and more and more glass walls. But despite all this squash does remain a sport for *doers* rather than watchers.

The good news, however, is that, believe it or not, squash need not necessarily be a case of 'do and die'. It is in fact perfectly possible to play squash without getting squashed all the time. And that's where this book aims to be of help. Over the years, many of the old sweats have developed a range of techniques, which for obvious reasons, they've tended to keep very much to themselves, known as 'Survival Squash'. Very few of these old campaigners, of course, would admit to using these methods, some of which, at first sight, may seem a bit underhand. The fact is, though, that they have helped a great many practitioners of the art of squash rackets to live to play another day. And they can do the same for you, too.

Needless to say, mastery of the knacks of Survival Squash doesn't mean being able to bury the ball in the nick any time you choose. If you can do that, there's not much else you need to know. This book is not aimed at the sort of player who, without a bead of sweat ever appearing, stands there effortlessly boasting the ball off a multiplicity of walls for hours on end, giving a whole new meaning to the word trigonometry. It's designed rather for the sort of player whose four-wall squeeze boast is not all that it might be; or perhaps even for those club 'rabbits' who feel they're having to spend too much of their time digging the pillock out of the back of the hutch.

As already indicated, many of these techniques are unorthodox. But then, as we all know, very few of the greats – not least the legendary Hashim Khan – every played textbook squash. They all had their little idiosyncrasies. Indeed, this may just be what gave their game the edge. It could be the same with you.

So if the knack of the nick has so far eluded you, if your middle name is not Khan, if you often wonder what it must be like to be fit, take heart. There are other ways of winning. It's not just former barefoot ballboys, reared on the North West Frontier, who have discovered the knack of playing without getting knackered. With the help of this book, you too can be an Unsquashable.

○ RULES OF SQUASH ○ THE NICK

The harder you try to hit the nick, the less likely you are to hit the nick

The nick never comes in time

You are more likely to hit the nick by luck than by judgement

Most 'nick' shots don't hit the nick

It's easier to hit the tin than the nick

You never hit the nick when you really need to hit the nick

It's more likely to land in the nick when you are not trying to hit the nick

You hit the nick more often in practice than in a match

1 Know the Game

'I can't help it, I just like beating people!'

Squash player quoted in The Times, *April 1983*

The first thing the Survival Squasher should get clear in his mind is the precise nature of the game. Squash, more than any other sport is about one thing – WINNING. Vince Lombardi might well have been talking about squash when he said 'winning isn't everything; it's the only thing'. For squash is the ultimate competitive game, and it's not played 'for fun'.

This means you're going to find yourself up against some pretty tough customers. Don't be misled by appearances. Off court most squash-players don't look much different from anybody else. Many of them are quite mild-mannered. Make no mistake, however. Though they may seem perfectly human at the bar, even the meekest of them invariably turn into blood-lusting monsters when they step into the pit. Almost without exception, squash players deep down (or, in some cases, not so deep down) are power-crazy egomaniacs, with a profound inner need to dominate at something. The squash court is where they fulfil that need. Don't believe any of that nonsense they may give you about playing the game for the exercise, or to forget the office, or to get away from the wife. The fact of the matter is that they come to the club in search of a *victim*. These are people who, if they weren't executives, or housewives, or taxi-drivers probably would be public executioners. They don't just want to kill the ball; they want to kill *you*.

Why else would they take up a game of such diabolical cunning and no-holds-barred violence, played in a confined space with potentially deadly weapons and offering unrivalled opportunities to crush and humiliate the opponent. There's more than just a ring of truth to the catch-phrase 'Give blood; play squash'.

Indeed, the term 'sudden death' takes on added meaning when applied to squash. The fact is, you can die out there. And people do from time to time. Even the ball is a potentially lethal weapon – we all know what can happen if you get one in the eye.

So it's certainly not going too far to say that when you enter the battle area, your demise is, at the very least, your opponent's *subconscious* objective. Once that door shuts behind you, his aim will be to crush you mentally and physically, to have you jibbering like an epileptic, begging for mercy, to leave you in pieces all over the floor so that the next people on court will have to wipe away the blood before they can start the game.

(In theory, of course, squash is not actually a 'contact sport' – but no one who has played the game takes this notion very seriously.)

It's surely no accident that the game's greatest exponents have turned out to be those fierce Pathan warriors from up around the Khyber, mostly called Khan, marksmen to a man, who can all hit the nick at twenty paces every time even in the dark and who, you would surely find, are all probably related to the great Genghis himself if you could trace them back far enough.

It's essential, therefore, for the Survival Squasher to discard any 'Baron de Coubertin' notions he may have about 'taking part' being the most important thing. This definitely does not apply to squash. Certainly, there may have been a time when it was a game for gentlemen – though in fact it is thought to have originated around the debtor's prison in Fleet before Harrow School took it up. But these days, it's unquestionably a game for players rather than gentlemen. So don't expect too many offers of 'Go on, Jack. Take a let. I'm sure I distracted you.' It's more likely to be 'A let? You must be joking.'

Of course, there are still a few clubs like the Landsdowne, Queen's and the RAC where you can find gents in blazers and striped ties reminiscing about that historic occasion when the Bengal Lancers played Peshawar Premium B. But at most clubs today the game is rather less hallowed, with a predominance of T-shirts and jeans at the bar and discussions tending to revolve around how 'City' are doing rather than what's doing in 'the city'.

These conversations can actually be rather deceptive. The tendency is to claim 'we're only here for the beer', to pretend that the only reason you play the game is because you enjoy replacing the lost liquid, rather than because you enjoy sweating it out.

Mention the league ladder and the response will tend to be 'I don't know why we bother with it'. But bother about it you can be very sure they do. A comparison might be made with tennis clubs where any attempts to get a league or a ladder going invariably fizzle out: or the thing never gets off the ground. By contrast, there can hardly be a squash club anywhere which doesn't have its ladder or its league. As we've said before, even though they may do their best to disguise it squash players are intensely competitive. They like to be graded, to have their place on the grid. Victory is all. Of course this also applies to the female of the species. The girls have taken up the game with a vengeance – as many an innocent male has discovered to his cost. And though, for the sake of convenience, this book mainly uses the masculine pronoun and avoids terms like 'Survival Squasheuse', most of what's said is equally true for both sexes.

Squash, then, is a case of squash or be squashed. But what the Survival Squasher has to learn is that there's more than one way of going about it. A talent for brutality is not the only way to succeed. And brute force can be effectively countered. There are survival skills to help you cope with every eventuality. Even it you find yourself up against the local butcher – the one with hair growing out of the palms of his hands, biceps on his ears, and forehand drives like Exocet missiles – the confident Survival Squasher needn't be too worried about the prospect of going home from the club in a wooden box.

Even the most fearsome opponents have their weaknesses – the main one being to assume that everything is decided out there on the court. The Survival Squasher, however, very often picks up his points *off* the court – in the locker room, at the bar afterwards, over lunch the next day. This is where he can be at his most devastating. Of course you also need to know how to hold your own when you step on court with the flesh-eating monster. But it's often elsewhere that you inflict the real damage.

Sometimes this may mean resorting to methods that not everyone would describe as fair and square. But knowing what he does about the true nature of the game and about the psychology and motivations of most squash players, the Survival Squasher shouldn't feel too many qualms or guilt about some of the methods he may be forced to employ. Remember, all is fair in love and war, and on and off the squash court.

○ RULES OF SQUASH ○ SHOTS

Better to hit the right shot off the wrong foot than the wrong shot off the right foot

The best stroke is a stroke of luck

The easiest shots are the ones you muff

Your flashiest shots cost you the most points

You will play your best drop-shots when your opponent is at the front of the court

If the whole of the court is open and your opponent is in the corner behind you, you will hit the tin

You are more likely to win the point by mishitting the ball than by playing the correct shot

2 The Club

'One could only get into the court by walking along the beams of the roof, and there was no gallery'

John Horry describing the first squash court in the United States

In order to be able to exploit his skills to the maximum, the Survival Squasher must give very careful thought to choosing his (or her) club. Since a good deal of your playing will be done *off* the court, it's important to pick a club where the environment is suitably congenial – perhaps the sort of place that's basically a pub with a few squash courts attached, where the regulars who talk about a 'stiff one' before the match mean a double Scotch rather than a hard knock-up.

Before coming to a decision, it's worth spending some time looking around at a variety of clubs and at their members and above all *listening*. The sounds of squash can be very indicative. Paradoxical as this may seem, what you need is the sort of club where the prevalent sound is of rackets bashing against the plaster and of flesh and bone crashing against walls and doors. If all you can hear is the steady squeak of rubber on maple, it's more than likely to mean that the place is full of the sort of precision players whose angled geometry defies comprehension.

Naturally you don't just want a club that's full of rotten players; that would simply reflect badly on you since all clubs acquire a certain reputation. It's important that, at the very least, the Club Team should be able to hold its own against the other clubs in the area.

The size of a club is often a good pointer. Though there's something to be said for the small, rather exclusive, Private Members Club, the Survival Squasher tends to be happier in a club which is big enough to get lost in, thus affording him some scope for manoeuvre. And if the club is rather larger it will at least tend to throw up a few players who can defend the club colours – even if the rest of the membership regard squash basically as a excuse for drinking.

Not that the club should be so big that is open to all-comers. Any self-respecting club has a proper waiting list – though how long applicants have to stay on the list, or indeed whether they go on it at all, is an obscure process which most clubs prefer to keep dark. The fact is that some people will always be on the waiting list – even if they had their name put down at birth. Others, mysteriously, will be spared this indignity. This is often because some clubs like to restrict membership to a certain kind of person. Thus you find clubs which are more or less comprised of solicitors, or of secondhand car salesmen, or of stockbrokers – most of whom go there simply to talk business.

A good way of finding out how active a club actually is can be to check how many divisions there are in the league or how many names on the ladder and then to divide those figures into the numbers of paid-up members. It is also worth dividing the number of courts into the number of members. These two tests should provide a fairly good indication of how much playing *really* goes on.

They also should provide an indication of how easy it is to get a court. Ideally, for the Survival Squasher, this shouldn't be *too* easy. Not being able to get a court is, in fact, a perfectly acceptable excuse for not playing. And the higher the ratio of people to courts, the more difficult this is likely to be. Fortunately, there are very few clubs where getting a court is *not* difficult – at least at the peak playing times. Incidentally, the fact that a club doesn't have enough courts needn't necessarily affect its prestige. One of the most exclusive clubs in the world, Jesters (membership by invitation only), does not have a single court. They just play on other people's.

You should also check out the standard and layout of the courts. Avoid clubs where all the courts have glass backs, closed circuit TV and large minstrels' galleries, or where all the courts are built around the bar to provide entertainment for the drinkers. What you really want is a club with a few back courts where you will not be easily observed. At some clubs, you'll find that the courts are actually in a separate block from the clubhouse; and this can be an even better bet for the Survival Squasher.

These back courts should preferably be a bit ropey, dimly lit, in need of a coat of paint, with a wooden makeshift back and with openings above the sidewalls so that ball can escape easily to neighbouring courts or get lost in the rafters. This will ensure that the better players stay away from them. And this, indeed, is why you don't want a club with too many rotten players – or, for that matter, other Survival Squashers: this simply leads to everyone competing to get on to the back courts, and perhaps forcing

you into the limelight of the show courts. And humiliation, of course, is all the greater for being public.

To sum up, you need a convivial club with a few good players and a fair-sized membership, where standards are perhaps not all that they might be but, there again, not too low. People should at least know the difference between an angle and a boast and, in a few cases, even be able to play one.

The club has also got to be the sort of place where you feel at home. The atmosphere in most clubs is usually pretty apparent as soon as you walk in. It shouldn't take long to suss out whether the stress is on the social side or on the playing side; whether the owner makes his money out of the snooker table and the slot machines or out of the court and the lighting fees; whether there's a resident barmaid or a resident professional; whether the prevalent smell is of beer and cigarettes or of burning rubber and freshly spilt blood.

Remember, too, that squash for the Survival Squasher is a *long* game. Not that he'll be spending two hours on court at a stretch, but rather that he'll be spending a fair amount of time hanging around *off* the court. So the right sort of surroundings are very important: you need a decent bar and restaurant facilities, and also one or two alternative recreations to squash, like a television set, darts and video-games.

There is no perfect club despite the fact that the range of choice is immense: you can find squash courts all over the place – in palaces, factories, private homes, ships, ski resorts, casinos, leisure centres, and also attached to tennis, cricket and golf clubs. However, to help give you a rough guide to selecting *your* club, here's a rundown of some of the more obvious possibilities.

○ THE CORPORATION SPORTS COMPLEX ○

Not exactly a 'clubman's club'. Invariably enormous – offering badminton, dancercise, sauna, swimming, gymnasium, trampoline, weight-training and sundry other activities as well as squash. What they call their 'squash club' is usually a rather random collection of individuals most of whom hardly know one another. This, however, can be an advantage for the Survival Squasher who likes to keep his distance. Also, the sheer size of the place affords the Survival Squasher plenty of scope for ducking around the complex pretending that he's doing other sports. Good value (i.e. cheap). Easy to join. And there won't usually be too many people around who know something about the game to watch you play. Surprisingly, this is often where the local international works out – so you can at least claim to be a 'clubmate' of Hiddelydiddely Zaman.

○ THE PRIVATE MEMBERS' CLUB ○

Altogether more exclusive, often of long-standing and with fading photographs of ancient teams in blazers and flannels on the walls. The sort of club where they all say two-love, rather than two-nil. May be privately owned, but will be run by The Committee. Not a bad place for the Survival Squasher – if he can get in. Has good social cachet – with a fair sprinkling of old school ties at the bar. Most of the members can usually play a bit – but this need not matter too much. The fact that the club is run by The Committee means that if the Survival Squasher gets in with these individuals, he can usually keep himself busy organising things (doing the league chart, arranging bridge nights and club dinners, or putting up notices saying 'No hob-nailed boots beyond this point' or 'Only *non*-marking balls to be used'). When it comes to playing, there's the advantage that many of the old prewar courts don't have spectators' galleries and are frequently having to be repaired.

○ THE HYPER-EXCLUSIVE ○

A smaller, even more select club, often with a name to match – something like 'Goggles' or 'Blazes'. If he can wangle a membership, this is the sort of place can often suit the Survival Squasher very well. The fact that the club is so small means that there is no league – only a ladder. And this will have long since fossilised since everyone knows who is better than whom. So members will long since have reached the very wise conclusion that there's not much point in actually bothering to play.

○ THE UPWARDLY MOBILE ○

A club that's going up in the world – the squash world that is, rather than the social world. All facilities to SRA standards; full-time professional; shelves full of trophies; constant state of expansion, adding on a new court approximately every six months; painters in permanent residence, so that you wouldn't know there was such a thing as a marking ball. Squash, in short, is 'what really matters in life'. Not ideal, therefore, for the Survival Squasher. The only possible advantage is that this sort of club, with 'strength-in-depth', plays a lot of matches, thus giving the Survival Squasher the chance to make his name as a marker or referee.

○ THE MONEYSPINNER ○

Ultra-modern, run by an entrepreneur who put it up during the squash boom of the seventies in the belief that he was going to make a killing. He's certainly doing his best. You pay for everything – membership, court charge, booking fee, lighting. Then there's the shop, sauna, hydro, ball-warming machine, snooker, darts, one-armed bandits, juke-box, and a variety of vending machines – 'vending' being the operative word. All perhaps a bit too brazenly commercial. He even has advertisements on the tin. The Survival Squasher, however, could do worse. These clubs are often biggish, giving him room to move around. And the fact that the proprietor put the place up fast and cheap means that it's now tending to fall apart, with the result that there are always one or two courts out of action. Even so it can be a bit much, even for the hardened Survival Squasher, to see the omnipresent owner gloating as he coins it out of other people's suffering.

○ THE PAY AND PLAY ○

Same sort of idea. A big-city club for people who can afford it, put up by some entrepreneur or conglomerate. Not a bad bet for the Survival Squasher, with its constantly changing clientele of international executives, diplomats and out-of-towners. This means they probably won't be around long enough to suss out the Survival Squasher – particularly as they tend not to hang around the club; they do their drinking elsewhere. The fact that the Survival Squasher is always at the bar when they put in an appearance will simply lead them to assume that he spends a lot of time at the club and is, therefore, probably a bit of a player. Another advantage is that a fair number of them are likely to be

foreigners, probably Americans, who can't really play (or who play 'hardball'), and are thus all good potential victims for the predatory Survival Squasher.

○ THE SQUASH 'N' NOSH ○

More of a salad bar or a pub with grub than a squash club. Not that the regulars make much of an attempt to pretend otherwise, though they may flail around for twenty minutes or so to 'work up an appetite'. But the real reason they come is for the 'light lunch', to talk business and to booze. The courts are simply there, in full view of the bar, to make them feel less guilty as they tuck in. Surprisingly enough these clubs often employ a resident professional: the regulars enjoy watching him down there in the pit sweating it out (on his own). It reminds them that there are worse ways of earning a living. Unfortunately, however, this is not the sort of club which is likely to enhance a Survival Squasher's reputation.

○ THE COMBINED CLUB ○

Here squash has teamed up with another activity – often badminton. So not a bad choice for the Survival Squasher, who can spend his time flitting between the two sets of courts pretending at each that the other is *really* his game. (You'll need to keep two sets of gear in your holdall – squash gear for badminton, and badminton gear for the squash court.) Another combination is where a squash club has been tacked onto a cricket club or onto a tennis club to keep them ticking over during the winter. This is perhaps even better: the Survival Squasher can thus spend all winter at the bar yearning for the start of the cricket season, and all summer in the pavilion eagerly waiting for the squash league to start up again.

○ THE COMPANY CLUB ○

A group of people at work who have banded together to persuade the management to put up a prefabricated court in the firm's basement. Not the sort of club for the Survival Squasher. Office colleagues of yours who don't play will come along to sneer when they get back from the pub at lunchtime. And they aren't going to believe you when you tell them that foldaway courts with wooden walls don't really suit *your* game. Still, there may be no harm in joining; you should be safe enough – the fact is that the court will always be fully booked through the lunch hour, which is precisely when you will want to play.

○ THE FAMILY AFFAIR ○

A sort of leisure centre for 'little ones'. All Coca-Cola and Croques Monsieur. Sometimes feels more like a crèche than a squash club. Designed for families who believe that 'the family which plays together, stays together'. Obviously not a good idea, therefore, if you 'play squash' in order to get *away* from the family. But otherwise not a bad bet. True, that juke-box always playing the same song, the smell of hamburgers and the bar-stools all sticky with ketchup can be a bit tiresome. The advantage, though, is that you can spend most of your 'playing' time on court 'teaching' the youngsters (until they start getting too good for you).

○ THE 'FRONT' CLUB ○

Here the squash is really a front for some other activity – like wife-swapping or do-it-yourself (where the 'players' spend most of their time rebuilding, repairing or refurbishing the club premises and then holding parties to celebrate each new accomplishment). The Survival Squasher may well find a few kindred spirits here.

○ THE COUNTRY CLUB ○

An American-style leisure and social club in the countryside, usually centred on a converted manor house. All kinds of facilities – but you can join just for the squash. The advantage of these places is that, with all the other activities going on, the Survival Squasher has the room for manoeuvre he needs. The disadvantages are the rather high fees and the fact that these clubs are not taken all that seriously by 'real' squash players.

○ THE COUNTRY HOUSE CLUB ○

Not to be confused with the Country Club. This is simply an old country house where the original owner had a squash court built in. Now, at the current owner's invitation, a group of chums are allowed to use the court and they've formed themselves into an informal sort of club. Good snob value for the aspiring Survival Squasher. The problem is that membership tends to be by invitation only and that your playing abilities may well come in for uncomfortably close scrutiny.

○ THE SINGLES BAR ○

A youngish club with an approximately equal male/female ratio. A sort of 18-30s club with squash courts attached. More interest in who is sleeping with whom than there is in the league. And more interest in getting a bar extension for party nights than there is in extending the playing facilities. The disco will be the main event of the week. Not a bad choice for the Survival Squasher – if he can stand the pace *off* the court.

○ THE CLUB IN THE COUNTRY ○

The sort of club that's found in remote rural areas, consisting perhaps of just a couple of not-quite-standard courts, and where they tend to make up their own rules and have their own special ways. Probably a bit too much of a closed circle for the Survival Squasher, but not the sort of club to be dismissed lightly. Often these yokels' match records are not at all bad – they invariably lose away but are more or less unbeaten at home. The fact is that no one else has ever mastered those converted barns which they pass off as squash courts (and which tend to have more ledges than a Real Tennis court). Many a young ace has fallen victim to their irregular concrete floors, bulging walls, low ceilings and dim lighting. And as if that wasn't enough there's always the local cat who's been specially trained to dart along the rafters at key moments.

○ RULES OF SQUASH ○ THE BIG POINTS

All points are important, but some are more important than others

When you start thinking about the score, you are more likely to lose the point

The more crucial the point, the more likely you are to screw it up

The more important the point, the more times you will bounce the ball

At 9-9 in the fifth you will stoop to depths you would never have believed possible

You can lose from being 8-0 up

The hardest point to win is when you're hand-in at 8-all

If it's match ball, it's easier to play catch-up than to win that match ball

3 The Survival Style

'We are not interested in the possibilities of defeat'

Queen Victoria to A.J. Balfour

It is just possible that the previous chapter may have given you the impression that the Survival Squasher tries to avoid actually playing if he possibly can. This is an impression that wouldn't be wholly wrong. The trouble is that, usually, he (or she) possibly can't. As we said at the outset, squash is a *participant* sport and even the most expert Survival Squasher can rarely get away without playing altogether. So even if you play what is basically an off-court game, it is essential that you also are able to hold your own in the pit.

We'll be discussing actual playing tactics and techniques – the winning ways of Survival Squash – in more detail later in this book. But a word should perhaps be said at this stage about the trump card in the Survival Squasher's game. This could be summed up as not so much the capacity to win as *the capacity not to lose*.

To understand this better, it is perhaps worth going back to first principles. We established earlier that the principal objective of the game is to crush and humiliate the opponent. It follows, therefore, that an opponent who does not achieve this invariably will feel that he has failed. He may win, but it will be a hollow victory.

So the key thing for the Survival Squasher to remember is that however vanquished he may be, he shall never *appear* to be vanquished. His opponent may romp through the match taking the first 27 points. But as they step off the court, you'd never guess it. The Survival Squasher will have saved himself by his sheer indomitability. His style and confidence remain intact. As they say in American football 'a team that won't be beat, can't be beat'.

What is the secret? How does the Survival Squasher manage to keep his head up when better players might be humbled and bowed? The most common method used by the Survival Squasher is to convey that, for him, squash is not the be-all and end-all. Not so his opponent, for whom squash will most probably be an expression of one of life's primary urges.

The Survival Squasher makes it clear, however, that for him squash is very much a secondary activity. Thus it doesn't very much matter whether he wins or loses.

He must convey this right from the outset – starting with his clothing. This may mean, for instance, wearing his Ralph Lauren polo shirt, or perhaps turning up in what is basically a tennis outfit, or in rugby kit, thus implying that squash is not really *his* game. (If you can contrive to get a faded rose of England or some other arresting insignia stitched on to your shirt, then so much the better.) As a matter of fact, 'downgrading' the

game in this way very much ties in with its origins at Harrow, where 'squash' was played with a soft 'squashy' ball just to warm up while waiting to get on with the 'real' (hardball) game – rackets.

To sum up, if the worst comes to the worst, the Survival Squasher can bank on having one extra shot in his locker: he possesses that rare skill of turning even the worst defeat into a sort of victory *simply by the way that* he loses. Thus the Survival Squasher must always be seen to lose gamely and with style. He doesn't skulk around the back corners in a vain attempt to excavate and return the ball. He doesn't lower himself to chasing after points. He stays poised on the T, even when he has no business to be there, taking whatever opportunities he can to hit that 'special' shot that he's been practising (perhaps the one that knocks out the light-bulb) – without, of course omitting to congratulate his opponent (albeit in a slightly patronising way) on all his perfect-length winners to the back corners.

The fact that you make no attempt to retrieve your opponent's best

shots will deprive him of the greatest pleasure he can get from the game – namely, your physical destruction. Indeed, as he machine-guns the ball up and down, he may take more out of himself that he does out of you; and this can be extremely demoralising for him, as you continue to hug the centre of the court, perhaps bouncing up and down on your toes. He'll soon start asking himself if you're both playing the same game. He may even go off *his* game as you just nod amusedly at all his brilliant shots as if you know something he doesn't.

Obviously this is an extreme example, the Survival Squasher will often be able to get into the game more (and we'll show you how later). But it does illustrate the ultimate strength of the Survival Squasher's game and demonstrates how, even when the run of the ball is against you, you can still put pressure on an opponent. What have I got to do, he will ask himself desperately as you continue unperturbed, still giving that confident little tap on the wall with your racket before service (on those rare occasions when you're hand-in).

At times you may find yourself up against an opponent who will want some sort of explanation for your devil-may-care approach to the game and for your apparent lack of concern for the score. One way to provide this is by wearing a certain amount of strapping and bandages. Not all that much need be said. You simply grit your teeth or gasp audibly from time to time as you stretch for a ball, allowing him to believe that you must be in considerable pain. He may even start to feel guilty and hit a few down (which should cause you to ask, with apparently genuine concern, if there's anything the matter). Even if this doesn't really come off, your wounds should at least leave him in no doubt that you've been playing some pretty tough games of squash lately. And, with any luck, this may persuade him to keep a safe distance from you.

The use of such trappings once again indicates the immense importance of dressing the part. But though the Survival Squasher's gear may be a bit unorthodox at times, it should never allow anyone to think that you are making light of the game. Squash may not be your *first* game but it is, for you, a serious business, one which fortunately, has not yet succumbed to the commercial razzmatazz of tennis. Thus you do *not* appear with advertising slogans all over you. And you don't wear your T-shirt with 'Kill' written across the front (however descriptive you feel this might be of your (very occasionally) deadly front wall nicks). And you do not go in for gimmicks, like that machine for warming the ball that plugs into your wristwatch, or by wearing a squash glove or an eye guard (the mark of the pansy).

One of the most effective approaches to gear can be to 'dress down' for the game, making out that you're a bit of a leftover from an earlier era. The squash 'boom' of the seventies has clearly passed you by. You just dress the way you always did – baggy shorts and faded whites, or perhaps that creamy colour, and preferably made of a sort of flannelly material – all designed to indicate that you may perhaps know a bit more about the game than meets the eye. The impression conveyed should be that you've been around and have hit an awful lot of small black balls in your time – on occasion in some pretty remote places. This can be effectively indicated by the odd stray remark like 'The game's never been the same since they stopped using the old Silvertown ball', or by prominently displaying in the front corner your towel bearing the legend 'Gezira Sporting Club, Cairo'. Incidentally, if your opponent is the type who plays a bit of a front wall game with delicate drops to the corner, there's no reason why you shouldn't cramp his style a bit by spreading your gear about under the tin. The Survival Squasher normally brings with him quite a pile of bits and pieces, which he keeps stopping to rummage in – to change his elasticated knee-band or his resin pad or whatever.

The Survival Squasher's racket will usually be 'classically' fashioned – perhaps solid rendered ash, hand-made by Grays – with an old towelling grip that makes it look as if it's been a long long time since you last broke a racket. And for an additional touch of individuality, there's nothing like a few notches carved on the shaft in memory of the victims of some of your greatest shootouts; or maybe some bloodstains on the racket head; or even something like an unusual surface to the grip which, from time to time, you can menacingly rough up with your keys.

The Survival Squasher, needless to say, does *not* go in for those open-throated jobs made of hi-tech material, or for rackets with those funny square-shaped heads that are supposed to make the ball easier to get out of corners. And if his opponent, perchance, has one, the Survival Squasher can often manage to make him feel quite ashamed of it, stopping to examine his wonderweapon with bemused curiosity and putting on a quizzical 'amazing what lengths some people will go to' kind of expression. For most Survival Squashers, of course, there's only one way of digging the ball out of the corners – the old way – though they may not actually demonstrate this all that frequently.

○ RULES OF SQUASH ○ SERVICE

Service is the stroke you fight hardest to achieve, and the one you most easily throw away

The surest way to win a point on service is to mishit the ball

When you hit a high lob service that feels like a winner, it usually goes out

If, by chance, it's in, your opponent will say he wasn't ready

You'll do the same when he's serving

Although you can start serving from either box, you invariably start from the right

If he's going to serve overarm, he has violent intentions

4 The Opposition

'She had said he worked too hard, played too much squash, kept her short of housekeeping and was unhygienic . . .'

Report in the Daily Mirror, *26 March 1985 about a squash-player's wife suing for divorce*

Survival Squash is not just a question of knowing *how* to play. You must also know *whom* to play. It cannot be stressed enough that one of the keys to the success of the survival game is careful selection of the opposition. It takes the right kind of person to play Hunt to your Barrington, Laurel to your Hardy. So before we go on to discuss survival tactics in more detail, here are a few sketches designed to help you to get the measure of some of your potential adversaries:

THE RACKET-BREAKER

Half of the broken rackets decorating the wall above the club bar are his handiwork. Takes a positive pride in smashing his racket and rather assumes that the rest of the club hold him in awe because of his destructive prowess. He may, of course, just be a Survival Squasher who's found an effective – if somewhat expensive – way of interrupting his matches.

THE OLD COLONIAL

You name it, he's played there – in Rangoon, Peshawar, Cairo and KL. And if you give him half a chance, he'll tell you about his marathon match, back in 'when was it now', against the legendary 'King' Khan at the old Punjab Club in Lahore. Usually good for a pink gin or two, though, if you express an interest in how Heliopolis used to match up against the Gezira Sporting Club.

THE EXERCISER

King of the locker room, where he will demonstrate vast numbers of

press-ups and sit-ups before the game in an attempt to psyche you out. This usually means he's rather less good at hitting a squash ball. And even if he can, by the time you get on court, he's usually far too pooped to cause very much damage.

THE CAVEMAN

The archetypal primitive, motivated purely by bloodlust, who really ought to be kept chained up. You can usually tell him immediately by the way he comes on court, kicking the door shut, wielding his racket like a shillelagh, and then going round testing the strength of the walls before the game. Make sure you keep your distances when he raises his arm to serve – or the smell of his armpits will knock you backwards.

THE SCRAMBLER

More of a danger to himself than you. Most of his wounds are *self*-inflicted. Charges around going for everything and, as a result, invariably ends up with severe concussion or his head through the door. Even if you're losing, it's worth hanging in there. With any luck, he'll be carried off before the end of the match.

THE KNOCK-UP HOG

Believes in maximising his chances by not letting his opponent get his eye in during the knock-up. His usual technique is to play the ball to himself for a while, then suddenly to hit it hard at an off-guard opponent, allowing him to step in to retrieve it, and then to resume hitting the ball to himself, perhaps muttering: 'Oh, all right then. I'll carry on.'

THE ASIAN

Probably a difficult opponent since all Asians are good at racket games. As often as not he'll be Japanese – there are one or two at most Western clubs, posted to your bailiwick by their company for a season or two. Don't be deceived by their mild Oriental manners. They want to win as much as you do. And don't rely on your usual verbal ploys: they won't understand them so they won't have much effect. (Be especially careful is his name is Khan.)

THE BALL-WARMER

Believes the secret of success is to get the ball warmed to just the right temperature for *his* game and is, therefore, always surreptitiously warming it up between points. He will invariably have brought his own 'special' ball along and will insist on playing with it. If deprived of this ball, however, he just goes to pieces. Best tactic, therefore, is to try to lose it in the roof, and then watch his game fall apart.

THE TRIGONOMETRIST

All angles and reverse angles. Looks very impressive, and if there were prizes for keeping the ball going and hitting the most walls he'd get it. Fortunately, he often gets so carried away with his strokemanship that he neglects to play winners. And if you just play the ball along the wall there's a good chance he'll double hit or break his racket.

THE EXHIBITIONIST

Similar type. Often found in pairs. They'll both have superb touch and a great range of shots. And they don't really mind who wins the point. It's how the shot *looked* that counts (and how *they* looked playing it); and how many times it whizzed around the court before bouncing; and, most important of all, how many admiring gasps they elicit from the people watching in the gallery.

THE SLUGGER

Believes the game is all about how *hard* you can hit the ball, rather than *where* you hit it. Hits the kind of shots that drill holes in the tin and needs to have his racket restrung at least twice a week. Actually not such a fearsome opponent: his shots aren't so difficult to return (on the rebound) – if you can *see* them; and he often tends to wear himself out fairly early. You can also count on a fair number of interruptions to replace broken balls. (Always let *him* warm the new ball up – he can do it with about four thwacks.)

THE LOBBER

Lobs everything – cross-court, down the line, on service. His theory is that by doing this he's 'keeping the ball slow' so that it's 'more responsive' to his subtler strokes. Spends so much time lobbing, though, that he's forgotten how to play his 'subtler strokes' and his occasional drop shots all bite the tin. His tactics can pay off, however, when his opponent, dazzled by constantly staring up at the lights, begins to lose sight of the ball, and his patience.

THE RUGGER-BUGGER

Plays squash to get fit for rugby. The problem is that no one has ever really explained to him the basic differences between the two games, i.e. that squash is not actually a 'contact' sport. Will, therefore, spend a lot of time 'squashing' you against the wall in what seems to amount to tackling practice; or, working on his 'blocking' technique, making you run around him as he stands planted on the T like a barn door.

THE TENNIS PLAYER

The most dangerous part of his game is his almighty back-swing and straight-armed follow-through. Otherwise not too difficult an opponent: he invariably plays the ball straight down the court as if he's frightened that if he hits it wide at the side-walls it might go out of court.

THE CASUALTY

The Walking Wounded. Arrives wearing eye-protectors, a gum-shield and with assorted parts of his body heavily bandaged. But don't be fooled. The purpose of this may well be just to get you to go easy on him. Would he be playing if he was in such a bad way? So just tell him about your double hernia and your dicky cartilage and get on with playing your usual game. After all, if he's in such bad shape already he shouldn't mind collecting a few extra bruises as you swipe at the back of his legs.

THE ROOF-CLIMBER

The type who's always clambering round up in the rafters or getting people along from the other courts to form a human pyramid so that he can scramble up the wall in search of a lost ball. He'd probably be happier giving up squash and taking up rock-climbing.

THE MOANER

Always complaining about something. The ball is either too fast or too slow. A broken light bulb or a blinking tube makes it 'impossible to see'. It's 'almost suicidal' to play with so much moisture on the floor. A bit of a bore – but at least he provides you with a handy set of excuses if you lose.

THE SLINGER

Has been told it's best to use a 'loose grip', which means that all too frequently his racket will come flying in your direction. May, of course, be a bit of a Survival Squasher who has found that this is a good way of

making sure that his opponents keep their eyes on *him* rather than watching the ball.

THE WALL-HUGGER

Wears a Barrington moustache and plays 'clingers' up and down the wall all the time, expecting you to do the same. Gets very upset if you try a little cross-court lob now and again so that he has to change sides and continue hitting down the *other* wall.

THE LOSER

The club masochist. Works at failure the way other people work at success. Would probably be very put out if he won a game. Always beating his breast and saying he 'can't understand it'. After all, he works at his game and he takes lessons. But he never seems to get any better. If it wasn't for the fact that he needs the exercise he'd have packed it in years ago.

THE RETRIEVER

The fittest man in the club. More of a long-distance runner than a squash player. Has seen all those marathon Barrington–Hunt matches, and aims to use the same tactics to grind you into the dust. He just keeps pooping the ball back to try to 'take the sting' out of your shots. Fortunately, he's so used to just getting the ball back that he can't put it away (or perhaps he just wants to prolong the rallies). The result will depend on whether or not *you* can put it away.

THE MUTTERER

Spends most of the time mumbling and cursing beneath his breath: 'Rubbish', 'Come *on*', 'Watch the ball', 'Get to it'. No need to worry – he never actually follows these instructions to himself. The mere fact that he's trying so hard is a guarantee that he won't succeed.

THE DRILLER

Frequently plays solo, booking the court for hours at a time (much to other people's annoyance) in order to rehearse his drills and set-piece combinations. His problem is that while he can do all these perfectly when there's no one else around, he can never pull them off in a match.

THE ZENNIST

An attractive opponent. Not much interested in the score and doesn't mind losing. He just puts his defeats down to experience and 'the learning process'. He's hooked on one of the new 'non-striving' squash theories and plays the sort of absent-minded game you'd expect from someone who's trying to let his subconscious do the work while he concentrates on 'listening to the ball'. Will probably want to go off for five minutes between games to 'park' his mind and to chant a mantra.

THE NICK-HITTER

His ambition is to transform his game by being able to kill the ball dead in the nick. Has pictures of Hashim Khan all over his bedroom walls and spends all his time practising hitting the ball into the crack. If he ever does manage to hit the nick even a fraction as often as Hashim could he'll be a formidable opponent. But no one at the club is too worried for the moment.

THE FLATTERER

Always giving you the benefit of the doubt and ever eager to pay tribute to your shots: 'Too good for me, I'm afraid.' Seems to get more pleasure from giving points than from winning them and frequently makes mistakes with the score in your favour. Either someone has told him you can turn into a caged beast in the pit and he's trying to appease you, or he's after something – your spouse perhaps.

THE SALESMAN

Also after something. Comes to the club to do business as much as to play squash. At some point (probably when you're feeling you may not stay the course) he's sure to interrupt the game to ask you if you're sure you've got enough life insurance. It may be worth letting him think he can sell you an extra policy: if you do, there's a fair chance he may let you take the match.

THE TANTRUM-THROWER

The club McEnroe. In his case, however, he has the tantrums but not the talent. Believes he has to be 'on the boil' to get his game going. He certainly needs an audience; and if there isn't one when he starts playing the sound of him cursing and bashing his racket against the wall will soon ensure there's a full house in the gallery. Fortunately for you he devotes a lot more energy to working himself up than he does to winning the points.

THE VETERAN

May look as if he's just having a final arthritic fling at the ball, but this 'Golden Oldie' is not to be underestimated. He learnt to play on an old fives court 'before the war' (no one's sure if he means the first or the second) and has picked up a range of sneaky unorthodox shots which, if you're not careful, will enable him to add you to his list of victims.

THE JUNIOR

Knows more about the game already than you are likely to learn in a playing lifetime. Best tactic is to try to turn it into more of a coaching session. So after he's been slamming winners into the back corners for a while, you say: 'OK. That looks pretty good. Now I'm going to put up some lobs for you. Let's see if you can put those away on the front wall.'

○ RULES OF SQUASH ○ STAYING THE COURSE

Whenever you think this must be hurting your opponent more than it's hurting you, he will be thinking exactly the same thing

The longest half hours of your life will be spent on the squash court

A rally that goes on, goes on and on

The rallies get longer as you get tireder

Three games of squash feels like five games of squash

The best moment in a match is when someone bashes on the door to tell you your time is up – especially if you are trailing 1-5 in the fifth

Losing is more tiring than winning

5 The Pre-Game

'The time before you play is worse than playing'

Richard Boddington

Vital as it is to be able to recognise the enemy, successful Survival Squash depends on knowing how to play him. The important thing to realise here is that the game often begins long before you both step on court. Many games are won or lost in the changing-room beforehand. And if he does his work well, the Survival Squasher can ensure that when the match actually starts he's already at a considerable advantage. So let's look at some of the principal phases of what is known as 'the pre-game' – arranging the match, locker-room chat, ball selection and the knock-up.

○ ARRANGING THE MATCH ○

This is your first skirmish with the opposition. Tradition has it – certainly when it comes to ladders and leagues – that it's the weaker player who issues a challenge to the stronger. But if this principle were followed, probably very few games would ever get fixed up at all: there aren't very many squash players who like to think of themselves as being inferior to their opponents.

For the Survival Squasher it's probably as well to get in there first – provided you can avoid sounding like too much of a toady. This has the advantage that the Survival Squasher can take charge of making arrangements for the game – thus putting his opponent in his debt right from the start. It also means that the Survival Squasher can ensure that the game is played on a court that is to *his* liking, rather than to his opponent's.

Every bit as important as *where* you play is *when* you play. Ideally, you want to pick a time which is 'just possible' for your opponent – though he'd 'rather not'. The way to do this is by proposing a variety of possible times, finding out the one which he 'could manage', but 'only just', and then insisting on playing then, as you suddenly remember that you are not free at any of the other times you proposed.

This is a tactic, of course, which may not be unfamiliar to him, and it is possible that he also may suddenly remember something else that he had on that evening. In this case you'll simply have to adjourn the discussion pending another go-around at a later date. But whatever you do – even if the discussion has to be adjourned several more times – never let him steamroller you into a time *he* proposes on the grounds that it's the only possible time *he* can play. If you hang in there long enough you should be able to agree on a 'mutually convenient' time – though this, needless to say, should be somewhat *less* convenient to *him* than it is to *you*.

One last tip: never give as an excuse that a particular time of day is no good because you can't get a court then. You might find that he, as it happens, *can* get a court; and there's a chance that this might turn out to be a glass-walled show court, just below the bar, perhaps even at a club that's entirely new to you. This, of course, should be resisted at all costs: any Survival Squasher worth his salt makes sure that he's playing on home ground, on that tried and tested old back court at his local club.

○ CHANGING-ROOM CHAT ○

This is really a continuation – at close range – of the previous conversation, and needn't necessarily take place in the locker-room. (In fact, should you find yourself playing an opponent of the opposite sex this is very unlikely to be the case.)

The aim at this stage is to begin to get him (or her) worried. Changing-rooms are actually a good place for this, since they make people nervous by reminding them of school. The best tactic is probably the breezy confident approach: the Survival Squasher will no longer be quite the same person who meekly offered to arrange the game. Quite the contrary. His aim now will be to convince his opponent that he's the sort of person who turns into a homicidal maniac when they put him down that unpadded call. (Some Survival Squashers even use a 'stooge' in the locker-room for this purpose – getting him to ask at an appropriate moment whether their opponent of the previous week is now out of hospital.)

Even if you don't go this far, make sure he notices the blood on your shirt, and the Indian clubs you keep in your bag to exercise your wrist. And even if you aren't actually all that fit, there's no reason why you shouldn't *look* fit – it's amazing what a little artificial sun-tanning lotion can do for your appearance. Another tip is to get there a bit before him, and then to starting doing sit-ups just as he comes in – counting loudly 'eighty-one, eighty-two, eighty-three . . .'

Above all, your mood should be *upbeat*. Remember the fundamentals of the Survival Style – you're going to be playing *for fun*, not *to win*. This is where you can, conspiratorially, offer him a swig from your hip-flask of some knee-weakening liquor. However reluctant he may be, don't let him refuse.'No go on. I always have two or three tipples before a game. It's pretty cold out on that court, you know.' If you do have a few yourself, however, make sure you don't swallow the stuff.

Some Survival Squashers go even further in their dirty-trickery – perhaps putting itching powder in his jock-strap, or grease on his racket handle. But that's probably going a bit too far.

At the same time as you're getting him worried, you should also try to disarm him: 'Don't know if I can give you much of a game. You used to be well up in the league, didn't you?' This tactic a) provides you with an excuse when you lose and b) makes your triumph that much greater if you win.

Of course, he may himself be no mean hand at the locker-room psyche. In this case, some Survival Squashers prefer to adopt an alternative approach: instead of cheerfully muttering 'Kill' under their breath, they hobble around the changing-room as if they were looking for their white stick. It can then come as quite a shock to their opponent that someone who seemed the essence of human frailty in the changing-room, can suddenly become such a monster in the pit.

You can also make good use of the locker-room to observe your opponent. Is he, for instance, the finicky type who brings his own coat-hanger along? Perhaps he's the sort who prepares for the game in a particularly ritualised way: most players have their little superstitions, like putting on the left shoe first or always using their favourite 'Lucky' locker. Upsetting his ritual can thus provide a first-rate opportunity to unsettle him. If you can get to his 'magic' locker before him, it could well be tantamount to starting the match 5-0 up.

One last point: as you get to the court, do make sure you get *your* token into the light meter first so that he is now *doubly* in your debt. (You also paid the booking fee, remember.)

○ THE BALL ○

You will probably find yourselves at odds once again over whose ball should be used. The fact is that a lot of players perceive it to be to their advantage if they can ensure that *their* ball is used. This also goes for the Survival Squasher. This, after all, could be his chance to insert into the game a ball that's about to burst and thus provide a crucial interruption at a key moment.

The usual pretext for objecting to using another person's ball is the colour of its spot. There's considerable one-upmanship associated with choice of dot colour. The general rule is that the person who proposes the slowest ball gets his way – even if this means playing with the double-dot super-slow used by the professionals in the middle of winter with the temperature on court at minus 5.

The only way to counter this is for the Survival Squasher to have about his person a variety of balls of different speeds. This means that even if your opponent insists, and you agree, to play with *his* ball, you can always swap it for an apparently identical ball of your own – perhaps using a little sleight of hand at the ball-warming machine or when you put the pill in your pocket. This is when some of the less scrupulous Survival Squashers – not content with simply getting into play one of their own favourite balls – go what might be considered a bit too far: they swap their opponent's ball for one *which has had its colour-spot 'doctored' to one speed slower than it really is.* This will more or less guarantee that your opponent will slam the first six points out of court by 'failing to judge' the pace of the ball.

○ THE KNOCK-UP ○

This should be the moment when the truth can no longer be concealed. Or can't it? Most players here either try to convince their opponent that they are more ferocious than they really are, or try to hide from him their sneakiest point-winning shots. Survival Squashers may adopt either approach, either determinedly trying to dent the front wall or pretending to muff shots as they secretly practise their deadly nick off the wood.

Perhaps the best rule of thumb is to try to give the impression that you're something other than you are. Thus, it is when you are feeling your least inspired that you show off your flashiest prize-winning boasts. But it must be admitted that the knock-up frequently degenerates into a competition to hit the ball hardest and to see who can bore the most holes in the tin.

The key thing about the knock, though, is not what you do while *you're* knocking up. It's what you do when *he's* knocking up. Take the opportunity to observe him carefully. Does he have a 'biased' grip? Is he playing with a brand-new racket and so keeping the ball well away from the wall – which, of course, is precisely where you will then proceed to play it. Does he look like a bit of a lob-and-drop player – in which case it might be worth your while bashing the ball as hard as you can to heat it up and so ensure that it will come rebounding down the court, so that you won't be 'caught long'.

Take the chance also to size up the court, reminding yourself of all those ledges and gaps in the roof which afford an opportunity to put the ball out of play for a good long while. And try to arrange your gear in the front corner in a way that's most likely to inconvenience and annoy your opponent.

You can also take the opportunity to get him even more worried than he was in the changing-room – perhaps looking up at someone in the gallery a couple of times and smirking; or running up and down the walls a few times.

Another option is to go in for straightforward physical intimidation. It's during the knock that some of the less scrupulous Survival Squashers take the chance to get in an early but perhaps decisive blow. This usually means stepping across court, swinging their racket like a scythe 'to intercept the ball' but, in practice, connecting with their opponent's anatomy on the grounds that he was 'hogging the ball'. And hogging the ball, as we all know, is something you should never never do during the knock-up.

One last tip: when you've finished the knock, do try to ensure that *you're* the one who spins the racket. You let him call, then either spin it in

your hand or just one and a half times – preferably, if he's the trusting sort, as he's getting out of his tracksuit. It amazing how many times it turns out that *you're* the one who starts off serving.

RULES OF SQUASH BALLS

'Non-marking' balls do

'Long-play' balls don't

No squash ball is ever *too* fast

No two squash balls play the same

A ball which suits your game perfectly will break during the match

The ball will split on the day you've forgotten to bring a spare

It will always break at the most critical point in a match

Although the British game is called 'soft' ball, anyone who's been hit in the eye by one knows this is not true

6 Match Play

'Get your retaliation in first'

Coach Carwyn James to the victorious British Lions during their 1971 series against the All Blacks

As we saw earlier, the essential Survival Squasher is one who, even in defeat, cannot really be crushed. Frequently, however, the Survival Squasher can go one better than that. If you manage to get your nose in front during the pre-game it's a pity to throw away your advantage during the match. And Survival Squashers have developed a range of techniques that can enable them to take on even the most fearsome opponents. In squash the best man (or woman) need not necessarily win – unless, of course, he (or she) happens to be you.

Now you may find this a little difficult to believe if you're the sort of player who gets tired putting on his kit in the changing-room; if you feel the main purpose of the side-walls is to hold the roof up, or for leaning on between points; if you've had difficulty in the past in finding the door after the match; if, when it's all over, you normally have to be put straight onto that traditional life-support system – the Guinness drip.

But, believe it or not, mastery of the basic on-court survival techniques can enable you to outgun even some of the better sharp-shooters in the club.

As we've said before, these are not the sort of techniques which will be found in the standard instructional manuals. These books tend to advise you to rely on your good-length shots and speed of movement around the court, prolonging the rallies to bring him to his knees and then playing winners out of his reach.

Unfortunately, however, these sort of tactics won't usually do you much good against the sort of super-fit player known for his 'wonderful range of kills' who sets about the game like the proverbial 'jet-propelled frog' as if he intends to hit the rubber off you as well as the ball and is determined that only one of you is going to leave that room alive.

In this sort of situation your salvation is much more likely to lie in applying some of the strategems outlined below, playing just within the limits of the law and managing at the same time to look very very innocent.

○ PREPARATION ○

This is all-important. First of all, do try to ensure that you're up against a suitable opponent. Don't take any notice of people who advise you to seek out opponents who are better than you are on the grounds that this helps you to improve your squash. The Survival School believes it's better to give your own ego a boost and, wherever possible, to play with your inferiors.

And do make certain that you are properly equipped. If it looks like being a game where you are going to have to take a lot of breathers, be sure to take along your racket with the 'detachable' head, or the extra light one that's been repaired several times and breaks easily when you smash

it against the wall. Take care, too, to see that the door is set to spring open at that crucial moment; and that your accomplice is stationed in the gallery to drop something on court whenever the situation becomes too desperate.

○ SCORING ○

Make a point, right from the start, of taking charge of the bureaucracy of the game and doing the scoring. This makes it so much easier to slip in the odd 'adjustment' to the score as you go along.

It also means that when it comes to a dispute over the score or over the rules, it's *your* interpretation as self-appointed 'marker' that will tend to carry more weight.

Being the scorer also provides you with an additional means of delaying the game when it suits *you*: you can always pretend to momentarily forget the score, and then embark on a lengthy reconstruction of previous points: 'Remember it was 3-1, and I was hand-in, and then there was that let . . .'

And, if he's the one who's pooped, being the scorer does give you the chance of 'boosting' your score quite a bit – for instance, hitting a winner at 3-1, and matter-of-factly announcing 6-1. If he's sufficiently fazed, with a bit of luck he won't even notice. And if he does – well, anyone can make a mistake; even a scorer normally as reliable as you.

○ CALLING ○

A vital technique to master if you're to make the best of all those 'was it/wasn't it' situations. Did the ball just touch the out-of-court line or not? Did it flick the top of the board? Was it perhaps a double bounce before your racket got to it?

The skill here is to sound convinced about your call even when you suspect it might be wrong, or even when you are damned sure that it's wrong. 'Not up', 'Out', 'Double Fault', 'Down', you say clearly and defiantly – except, of course, when it's *your* shot that hits the tin, in which case you may prefer to play on as if the ball *was* good.

If, however, your opponent takes it upon himself to do some calling, do feel perfectly free to cast doubt on *his* claims. Make sure he *earns* his points. There's no harm in looking slightly doubtful, even when he hits a clear winner, and asking innocently: 'That looked all right to you, did it?'

You won't however, want to contest every point. If it's a 'double', with the ball bouncing a good five times before you manage to get your racket to it, you may as well concede: 'I don't believe I did get *that* one up'.

○ DOMINATING THE 'T' ○

In conventional theory, the reason for holding on to the T is that this gives you the maximum chance of getting to a ball in every corner of the court. It's from the T – so the theory goes – that you can dictate play, chipping and lobbing your opponent around court and generally running the legs off him.

Survival Squashers also like to hang on to the T, because
a) it's the status position
b) it's the best place from which to *block your opponent* from getting to any corner of the court
c) it's the best place for preventing your opponent from getting a good view of the ball.

It's important, therefore, to establish right at the start who is going to hog the central position, and who is going to spend the match slinking around the back-court. This can involve a certain amount of pushing and shoving if you find yourself up against an opponent who doesn't realise that *his* place is *not* on the T. The Survival Squasher need have no qualms about using his racket if necessary. It's generally accepted as perfectly in order to soften up the opposition with a few gentle swipes as you tussle for possession of the central station.

○ STANDING YOUR GROUND ○

It's not just on the T that you have to stand your ground. The successful Survival Squasher must make it clear that he's the kind of player who can't be pushed around on *any* part of the court. So stand firm, sharpen your elbows, whirl your racket about as much as possible, play your backhands as if it's harvest time and develop a talent for getting in your opponent's way. Don't worry too much if he tries to counter with 'the Let' (a tactic which will be discussed in more detail in the next chapter).

Make it clear that if he's going to get at the ball, he's going to have to run *around you* – and a long way around if he's to avoid being blocked or tripped. It's important, also, to learn to place the ball accurately so that your opponent spends most of his time making these long detours.

Needless to say, when employing these tactics some subtlety is important. None of these moves should be done too obviously or seem too calculated. After all, gentlemen (and women) don't deliberately obstruct. As we've seen, however, there are a few *players* in the game now. And squash is, when all's said a done, a physical game. Just watch any two players competing to get in front of one another to play those front-court winners.

So it's inevitable really that in a game when you have to make so many split-second judgments that the odd mishap will occur. It's not always easy, in the heat of the moment, to decide whether to run at the man (and how hard) or whether to run at the ball. Hardly surprising, therefore, if the Survival Squasher finds himself doing the former from time to time. It's the same when you're lining up to play a splendid stroke which might just connect with your opponent before it hits the ball. Can you really be blamed afterwards for taking your chances?

○ THE INJURY GAME ○

As so often in squash, the secret here is timing. It's just when your opponent is stepping in to kill an easy ball that you suddenly pull up, moaning and clutching a hamstring.

When you're playing the injury game, always try to do the unexpected. You might, for instance, phone your opponent the day before, hinting that you're injured and that you may not turn up thus inducing him to anticipate a walkover. You then do show up the next day *at the very last minute* – just as he's about to go upstairs and order a pint. Be sure to express your surprise that *he* should be surprised to see you: 'You didn't really think I was going to jack out, did you?'

It's often necessary, of course, to equip yourself – with bandages and

plasters and so on – to give credence to your claims. And if you intend to have an attack of hay fever or one of your periodic fits, you may have to prepare for this in the early stages of the game by stopping from time to time to check your pulse, foaming at the mouth, wheezing and giving the occasional last gasp.

Props like bandages also can be useful in providing you with an excuse to leave the court now and again – allegedly to bind your wounds up again, but in reality to have a bit of a breather if your opponent suddenly hits a hot streak.

There will be times when you won't choose to come *back* on court – if, for instance, it looks as if his hot streak will last and the match is turning into a bit of a disaster for you. But even though this will mean forfeiting the match, it's worth remembering that the accomplished Survival Squasher can, on occasion, manage to leave the court a 'moral' victor. Once again, the key to pulling this off is timing, since it usually involves falling against your opponent's racket head just as he's looking the other way. You can then proceed to roll around in agony for a bit and finally hobble off the court saying: 'There are rules about dangerous play, you know. Before we play again, I'd like you to do something about that backswing of yours if you don't mind.'

○ THE TALK GAME ○

The principal use of this stratagem tends to be for distracting your opponent. Most of the time you can pretend to be talking to yourself; at least that's what you *claim* if challenged – explaining that when you muttered 'bastard' under your breath you were of course referring to your thumb which is giving you trouble and *not* – perish the thought – to your opponent. At other times, though, your remarks will not be quite so sotto voce – such as when you stop to exchange views with friends in the gallery (about your opponent) or to engage in a dispute with the marker.

Alternatively, you may prefer to address your opponent *directly*, chatting away and disturbing his concentration – especially if he's the type who obviously doesn't like being chatted to. What can sometimes be effective is to take him into your confidence, or to offer him a good business tip; he may then feel obliged to offer you some sort of reward and start hitting the odd ball down.

Even if he's reluctant to engage in dialogue, you shouldn't let this

inhibit *you*. Feel free to offer a running commentary on *his* game. You can either lavish praise on his efforts, calling out 'shot' to all of his best flukes and making *apparently* flattering remarks like: 'Interesting, that grip of yours.' Or you can be a bit more ironic, calling out when he hits it into the tin:

'What rotten luck'
'Nice one, Cyril'
'Same again, please'
'Thank you very much, squire'.

But perhaps the most useful sort of remark is when you can implant some seeds of doubt in his mind about his game which are going to get him wondering, and worrying, for the rest of the match: 'I know some people do play that shot off the wrong foot, but . . .'

○ GOING FOR YOUR SHOTS ○

Some shots, of course, are more important than others – with perhaps the most important being those which can cause Grievous Bodily Harm.

In handling this sort of shot, squash-players tend to divide into two types. There are those who, when their opponent is directly in their firing line, *don't* shoot and hope for the point that the referee would have given them if they *had* hit their opponent. And there are those who *do* shoot – as hard as they possibly can.

In many respects, taking the latter option would appear simply to be sheer common sense. The fact is that in the club game, as often as not, there is no referee; and the victim you've spared won't give you the point but will suggest playing a let instead. To ensure that there's no doubt, therefore, the sensible Survival Squasher often feels forced to let fly – just to make sure.

If you are going to go for the shot (and your opponent) it's also common sense to make the most of it. One valuable refinement is the 'check' before you play the stroke to deceive your opponent into thinking that you weren't going to hit the ball at *him*, but were going instead for one of your disguised cross-court lobs or were looking for somewhere *else* to hit it. And for the less scrupulous Survival Squasher, there's always the last-minute adjustment of the wrist – so that you send him in the wrong direction, i.e. *towards* your racket.

However, always remember your court manners and apologise profusely for any injury that may occur.

○ 'LINGERING' ○

A successful 'linger' can be the key to a great many points. When you've played what could be a winner into an open court, and you've got your opponent boxed in the corner, it's up to you to see that he can't get out of that corner in time.

Now it's true that the rules do say that, once you've played your shot, you must make *every effort* to give your opponent a fair view of the ball and complete freedom to play whatever shot he wishes. But, as every Survival Squasher knows, there are rules and rules. It's not unknown for players to hang back after playing their stroke. And to get away with it. Just how long you 'linger' rather depends on your opponent: is he the type who prefers to play on (even if one of you gets clear a little late sometimes) or is he the sort who insists on interrupting the game to claim lets over minor technical offences?

The secret of successful 'lingering', then, is to have a sense of proportion and not to go to extremes. With a bit of practice, the Survival Squasher should be able to play a shot that effectively 'snookers' his opponent and then to move away from the return ball a fraction or so late – though not so late that he gets hauled up for it.

○ CHANGING THE GAME ○

'Always change a losing game' is what they say. And if you should find yourself running around the court, desperately chasing the ball and scraping it out of the corners, then clearly something must be done about it. But the trick is not to change *your* game (there's not usually much you can do about *that*); but rather to change *his* game.

So if he just stands there playing perfect-length clingers up and down the wall, the best Survival tactic is to simply psyche and taunt him out of it:

'I know the defensive game is 'in' now, but this is ridiculous'.

Or

'We've seen you play to the back of the court; isn't it about time you let us see what you can do when you get to the front?'

Or

'It's all very well rallying all day, but I think the game is about hitting winners, don't you?'

(The reason *you* go for winners, of course, is that you *can't* rally all day.)

○ TAKING A BREATHER ○

This is an absolutely essential skill to be mastered when you're up against the sort of player who's fitter than you are, or where you find yourself in the sort of game where the rallies are lasting much too long. As we've seen, careful choice of court can be a big help here – it can hardly be counted as your fault if the ball tends to get lost in the rafters or keeps drifting over the wall to the next court.

Of course, the rules do say that play should be continuous. But there are some little interruptions that just can't be helped. Here are a few of them:

– tying shoelace
– losing contact lens
– having to wipe spectacles
– stripping off track-suit bottoms at crucial moments
– changing rackets (all too frequently)
– taping up the towelling grip on your racket handle

– towelling off between points (as in tennis)
– leaving the court to change ('I think my knicker elastic is gone')

– inspecting the walls for sweat, dust, loose plaster
– wiping the sweat off the floor (with *his* tracksuit)
– checking that the tin is still intact
– asking about *his* shoes ('Excuse me, but are you sure they aren't damaging the surface?')
– finding that the gear in the front corners is bothering you ('Let's clear the court shall we?')
– hearing things ('Are you sure that ball didn't tick the racket?')
– moving very slowly around the court
– stopping to check pulse

– getting cramp (if he won't allow you off the court, say you'll vomit)
– having to take a long-distance phone-call at a crucial point in the match
– getting summoned to move your car (which, as it turns out, *happened* to be double-parked in front of the car of the people who were on court just before you).

You can also do a great deal with the ball – or rather *without* the ball. There's many a Survival Squasher who's been saved by the ball:

– spot a ball on a ledge that you're sure is the one you lost last week, and start chucking your racket at it to get it down
– hit the ball out of court into the gallery
– bounce ball at some length between serves
– stop to inspect the ball ('Are you sure that ball is giving a true bounce?')
– between points, 'accidentally' knock the ball up the court and slowly walk after it
– allow the ball, by mistake, to drop onto your foot and roll into the far corner, so that it has to be picked up – preferably by him
– if the ball rolls toward you, pretend not to see it and let him fetch it (if he wants to get on with the game).

○ RULESMANSHIP ○

The Survival Squasher may bend the rules every now and again. But he should also know how to apply the rules – especially against opponents who clearly don't know the letter of the law.

The important thing, when invoking the rulebook, is to do so in a very matter-of-fact way, with no hint that you're trying to get something for nothing. The effect of a particular ruling may sometimes be regrettable (for him). *But the rules are the rules.* And *you*, at least, are in the habit of playing by them.

So there's no reason to feel guilty if you penalise him for foot-faulting every now and again. And if he tries to be decent and says 'turning' don't let the fact that he was trying to be helpful stop you from (regrettably) claiming the point.

But it's not just a question of *knowing* the rules. You must also know how to interpret them. Fortunately for the Survival Squasher there are a lot of grey areas which lend themselves to imaginative interpretation. There is, for instance, the rule which says that you must have complete freedom to play any shot you wish. But how much freedom is freedom? Certainly one interpretation of this rule should enable you to disallow quite a few of his winners; he may have *thought* he was well clear, but obviously he wasn't to know that you were going to play your reverse-angle triple-boast (with double pirouette) that needs the very complex wind-up.

○ RULES OF SQUASH ○ THE LADDER LEAGUE

In every league there are people who ought not to be

They will think the same about you

The person who was beaten by the person that you beat is the person who beats you

No one believes they're in the right league for them

Everyone was in a higher league once

You are more likely to be on the way down than on the way up

People above you on the ladder will make as many excuses not to play you as you will make not to play the people below you

And do make sure he doesn't try to put one over *you* with the rules. You do, for instance, get the odd 'clever clogs' who tries to claim a point rather than a let when his ball hits you. It's up to you to be on your toes and to point out that, even though it may not have looked from *his* angle as if the ball was going towards the front wall, it would, in fact, only have got there *via one of the other walls.*

If he keeps on trying to be clever, you need have no hesitation in throwing the rulebook at him and awarding yourself penalty points for his 'dangerous play', 'time-wasting', 'obscene language', 'wild follow-through' and, perhaps worst of all, 'arguing with decisions' (yours).

With this sort of character, you can justifiably feel free even to take a few liberties yourself with the rules – getting him for 'crossing the line of the ball' (even if it didn't actually disturb you); or pretending to give up as he moves to play his easy winner and then claiming the point because he didn't actually play the shot.

After all, if he's going to take liberties there's no reason why you shouldn't.

○ SERVING ○

Once again, timing is of the essence if you are going to capitalise on service. You need, for instance, to be able to deliver your serve just that split second before your opponent is ready (at the same time making it clear that you'll be giving short shrift to any 'Not ready' claims that he may venture to make).

Needless to say it's a bit different when you are *receiving* service. Here, it's a question of waiting with *your* call of 'Not ready' for just long enough to see how good his service was. There *will* be occasions when he muffs it and you will want to go ahead and play it.

When he serves a single fault another good wheeze is to look as if you're not going to take it, but to casually let the ball bounce on your dropped racket-head. *If*, by chance, the balls stays up and just pops on to the front wall above the tin claim that – though it may not have *looked* like it – *you certainly were playing the ball as good*. In fact, you can tell him, that particular shot – unorthodox as it may look – is one of your specialities.

You can also make your service work for you when you are feeling the pace a bit. Give the ball a good bouncing before you make your delivery. And if you really need to take a breather, there's no law against deliberately serving a single fault to give yourself a little more time to recover.

Another possibility is to shuffle to the wrong service box from time to time before realising your mistake. Your opponent probably won't twig what you're up to. After all, it's happened to most of us, that we've got so tired that we couldn't remember which side we were supposed to be serving from.

○ LASTING THE PACE ○

There's not a great deal that can be said about this – except that, however awful you feel you should try to disguise this fact from your opponent. Of course, this is easier said than done. There will be times when you have only the haziest notion of where the front wall is. And often enough you won't even *care* which is the front wall: *any* wall will do if you need something to lean against. It's in this sort of state that even the bitterest of foes have been known to call a sort of truce and have resorted to propping one another up through the final points of a marathon match.

Nevertheless, there is something to be said for trying to let your opponent think that this must be hurting him a damn sight more than it is hurting you.

So, if you are still able to talk, it can be worth trying to keep up what passes for a cheery flow of conversation. With a bit of luck this may convince him that, however knackered you may *look*, you obviously have more energy left than meets the eye. How else would you be babbling on like that? After all, talking is usually the last thing anyone feels like doing when they're on their knees and about to cough their intestines up . . . .

○ RULES OF SQUASH ○ ARRANGING LEAGUE MATCHES

You won't have his phone number

You won't be able to find it on the league chart

He won't want to play when you want to play

When you can both play, the court will be booked

You will end up by playing when neither of you wants to play

The person who rings up is more likely to lose

Most league matches are played in the last week of the month

7 The Let

'I spent a second trying to reach it by climbing through Cam's legs and ended up pathetically lying on the floor appealing for a let, but mercy came there none!'

Jonah Barrington

The Survival Squasher won't always win most of the points. But if he's worth his salt, he should see to it that he does win most of the lets. Survival Squashers were among the first to realise how the let had become one of the dominant features of the modern game. So much so, that at many of today's international matches, you could be forgiven for thinking that they were actually playing for lets instead of for points. The fact is that these days the let is no longer simply the gentlemanly arrangement that it used to be, when both players agreed to play a point again if – through no fault of either party – there was a collision or they got in one another's way.

The theory todays seems to be that if you can't win the point then by skilful use of the let you can do the next best thing and *prevent your opponent from winning the point.* Thus, even if you haven't a hope in Hell of getting to the ball, you give yourself another chance by claiming that, *but for him*, you could have done. In effect, this means that whereas the main aim of the game used to be to score the most points, the aim now seems to be to *prevent* one another from scoring points.

It is this development probably more than any other which has been responsible for transforming squash into a 'contact' game. The truth is, let's admit it, that a lot of those collisions are 'accidentally-on-purpose'. We've all come across opponents who collide *deliberately* so that they don't have to run a long way for the ball, or who make a point of colliding with an opponent poised on the 'T' who's just played a winner and thus claim a let. Players these days are getting up to all kinds of tricks, like hiding behind the other player and then claiming that they couldn't see the ball. Crudest of all, there's the player who, whenever he fails to play a winner himself, simply charges into his opponent from behind and then claims his let.

The result is that squash, at times, has come to resemble nothing so much as a game of tag – especially towards the end of a knee-buckling needle match. It's got to the point where whichever player finds that the ball is out of his reach automatically stretches out his hand to try to touch his opponent and claim his let while his weary opponent does his best to duck out of the way.

Another reason for the popularity of 'the let game' is that as well as preventing your opponent from scoring, you can also begin to *affect his game*. Hardly surprising if, regardless of where the ball is, you keep knocking him down and asking for the point to be replayed. As the old Serbian proverb goes: 'It may not be profit for me, but it's damage to him.' This damage, of course, is usually physical damage. Thus 'the let game' is a good way of softening up an opponent. And someone who has been charged in the back often enough may begin to feel that, instead of putting the ball out of his opponent's reach, he might do better to play balls that his opponent has some chance of getting.

Clearly, therefore, Survival Squashers have no choice but to master 'the let game' and to make sure it works to *their* advantage – even, at times, adding a few refinements of their own. Here are a few suggestions.

Before calling a let (when he's at fault), it's often best to play on and first see who wins the point. That's no reason, of course, to let *him* get away with any late let-claims. On these occasions, you'll simply have to pull him up: 'I don't mind what you call it, but if you're going to call it, call it – there and then, if you don't mind.'

It doesn't do any harm either to make it clear to him that he's got off lightly. 'If we'd been playing at international level, you know, that would have been a penalty point.'

It's also sound policy to look disbelieving whenever *he* asks for a let. No let should be easily conceded. All too often you'll find yourself up against some joker who claims a let when he hadn't a cat in Hell's chance of getting to the ball, but who makes a vague lunge at your feet and tries to explain afterwards that getting at these sort of balls is his speciality.

The only time when you might behave more magnanimously is when you are so many points ahead that you can afford to be generous. You can then ask him gallantly, when he least expects it: 'Do you want a let?' Remember, though, in squash you can never *really* be far enough ahead. If you do give a few away though, it may stand you in good stead later on when it comes to claiming your lets on those big points that may make all the difference.

Some Survival Squashers do go so far as to stage-manage some of their lets, by arrangement with an accomplice outside the court. Thus, at a crucial point in the match, they get distracted by a noise in the gallery or by a knock on the door.

And don't overlook the possibility of claiming you were distracted by your *opponent*: you find you hit the ball in the tin, and then claim it was because of your opponent's coughing.

Sometimes you may even find that it pays not to even 'justify' your let. When he plays a shot you can't get to, you simply pick up the ball and resume serving, as if there was no question about *his* guilt and *your* let.

It's amazing how much you can get away with by sheer gall: 'I'm sorry. I dropped my racket.' (Deliberately?) 'Do you mind if we play a let?'

There will be occasions when he *will* mind. But, nonetheless, it's often a sound tactic to ask innocently for a let even when there's absolutely no reason for him to give you one, thus interrupting a rally which was going his way. There are some opponents who will jib a bit at this. But in these instances, the Survival Squasher should stand no nonsense from someone who tries to protest that he 'would have won that point if we had been able to continue'.

In order to handle this sort of situation, you've got to make sure that your disputes drill is up to scratch. As we've said before, the Survival Squasher should be able to come out on top because most players don't really know the rules. It's often enough just to reel off a few official-sounding formulations about 'denial of fair view' 'stroke entitlement' etc, to deter him from taking you on.

It's actually that rule about 'fair view and freedom of stroke' which should get you the most lets. Can he really pretend that he made *every* effort to get out of the way (as the rules stipulate). If he had done, there's no question that you would have got to that ball easily.

Of course, you may take a slightly different view of this situation if *you* are the one who is doing the obstructing – especially if you're rather big and rather broad. Allowances have to be made – you can explain to your opponent – for a person's physique. It's hardly your fault that you're 6ft

4in and weight 18 stone. (You might also point out that in squash it's the short nippy players who are said to be at an advantage.)

If, on the other hand, *he's* the one who's reluctant to give lets then there's often not much point in arguing about it. You'll have to use other means of persuasion – like thumping him a few times. And don't limit yourself to friendly pushes in the back. Ram him in the kidneys. With some players it's the only way. (Be a bit careful with this tactic, though, if *he's* the one who is 6ft 4in and 18 stone.)

○ RULES OF SQUASH ○ COVERING THE GROUND

It's more tiring to go backwards and forwards than to go from side to side

Moving fast is only an asset if you move in the right direction

He who does the most running usually loses

Even though you play for the exercise you prefer your opponent to do most of the running

Running can slow you down

The court gets bigger and the distances greater as the game goes on

The quickest way of wearing out a pair of gym shoes is squash

8 The Battle of the Sexes

'If the ball comes down the middle of a court and he still won't move out of the way, you have to whack him with the ball once or twice and then he will move! Nobody likes to hit anybody intentionally, but if that's what happening, hit him once or twice – gently'.

Sue Cogswell

Traditionally, squash has been a predominantly male ritual – young warriors locking horns in an adjunct to the officers' mess. The ladies didn't really come in to the picture at all, even as spectators. Not like rugby, where devoted females have long been accustomed to stamping the touchline duckboards in their wellies, wearing the tribal colours round their neck and waiting patiently to comfort those wounded in battle.

But women never seem to have taken much pleasure in sitting around in chilly squash galleries watching their partner slashing away below. They apparently preferred to become squash widows instead, staying at home and grumbling that he was more interested in having his way down at the club then he was in having his way with them, perhaps consoling themselves that at least he wasn't having it away anywhere else.

These sexual analogies, by the way, are not incidental. The physical intimacy of squash and the deep passions involved have led more than one psychiatrist to speculate that the game is, in reality, a sort of substitute for sex. Certainly the toll which squash takes on the body inevitably means that, as often as not, it is a case of 'either/or'. As a woman receptionist at the Hampstead Club, quoted in the *Observer*, put it: 'They are much more interested in conquering each other on court than me off it.'

But things aren't quite what they were. Squash can no longer be considered a game reserved for 'hard men'. There is now no shortage of 'hard women' at most clubs.

It's true that some girls do just come along to keep tabs on their mate, or even to find one. But there are a fair number who are there to *compete*; and that doesn't just mean plopping the pillock back and forth with one another. All too many of them are looking for a victim – preferably male.

There can be few men playing in club leagues today who have not had the experience of coming up against a woman made of whipcord, determined to take it out on him and make his defeat that much more humiliating.

It all began innocently enough. It seems that a few men started to bring their wives or girlfriends along to the club for a drink. Then, in all probability, one or two chaps began getting the girl on court as a prelude to getting her into bed – little knowing where all this would lead. And it wasn't long, as we have seen, before squash had become a family affair, with women and children discovering a great new outlet for domestic aggression.

Clearly there's no turning the clock back now. The sexes have got to learn to live with one another on court – difficult as this may sometimes be. And it's a situation with which Survival Squashers of both sexes must come to terms. For obvious reasons this tends to be much easier for the girls than it is for the men. They are just not subject to the same pressures – most notably, the male squash ego. The advice in this chapter, therefore, is geared more to the male Survival Squasher, than to his female counterpart.

Perhaps the most important thing is to learn to recognise the enemy. Basically, there are two types of woman player. There's the sort who gets her main satisfaction from the game *off* the court – rather like the Survival Squasher. Indeed, the Survival Squashing male should not underestimate the importance of forging alliances with this kind of female of the species. This is the sort of woman who has given 'social squash' a good name. They probably joined the club just for the Saturday night disco and prefer to watch the men down below fighting it out *for* them rather than engage in combat themselves.

At the other end of the spectrum there's the sort of woman whose attitude to the game is distinctly 'anti-social'. This type of woman has no inhibitions about beating a man – even her husband. Quite the contrary. She's taken to squash to get her own back on the male sex in a sport that is all about domination and submission.

What's more *she can be very hard to avoid.* In squash you don't have the same ways of getting out of this sort of encounter as you do in tennis, for instance, where you can often solve the problem by playing mixed doubles. And in tennis, of course, if you do find yourself playing singles, it's easy enough to turn it into 'a hit', to patronisingly use your 'second serve', or even to 'let her win'. In squash, as everyone knows, no one 'lets anyone win' – not, at all events, in the league, which unlike the tournament does not keep the men and the women neatly segregated. Also, in squash, the same rules apply to both sexes. No scope, therefore, for pretending, as in tennis, that the woman's game is somehow inferior because they only play three sets instead of five. In the club league they too go the full distance – and can outlast a good many males in the process.

The physical qualities of these women should on no account be underestimated. Tough, ruthless, with the killer instinct of a spitting cobra, they're often physically extremely well equipped for the game. With their low centre of gravity and their weight concentrated around the hips, they can give you quite a bump when you have the misfortune to collide with them. And they're up to every trick in the book – with a repertoire that includes some very sneaky shots. There is, for instance, that classic female speciality – a highly unorthodox, imprcbably-looking drop cross-court kill to the front wall, that looks like a pretty awful shot when she plays it but which invariably catches you out.

In the early days, many men did have a stab at trying to cure them of this sort of thing, showing them how to play a more orthodox game; how to use the *strings* of the racket to hit the ball; and how to play it straight up and down the court, instead of having the ball come off the racket at all angles, winning points by sheer ineptitude.

It wasn't long, however, before men began to realise that this gallantry was proving, if anything, counter-productive. The girls were taking all their useful tips, no longer trying to play drop-shots with their opponent in front of them but they were still persisting in playing those unorthodox winners from impossible angles, often using the most unlikely parts of the racket. It was at this point that the truth began to dawn: the girls didn't *want* to learn to play a *decent* game, they wanted to win – at any price. And from then on it became clear to males that brute force and rat-like cunning had to be met with brute force and rat-like cunning.

The result is that these days, whatever the male on court may *pretend*, there's usually no quarter given. In fact it's often those battles between the sexes which are the fiercest, as is all too apparent from the distraught state of the contenders – damp-haired, pink-skinned, purple-faced and rubber-legged.

It's hard not to feel sorry for some innocent young male who finds himself in one of these no-holds-barred contests against the sort of predatory female who is on the women's team and forcing her way up through the league. The Survival Squasher should make no allowances for this sort of woman. She certainly wouldn't for him.

Of course it won't always be like that. There will be times when either or both players are on court simply to further their prurient interests. And there's no question that squash does lend itself to this sort of encounter – the physical intimacy of the game, the whole ritual of stripping off, of chasing one another round, of squashing each other into the corners, of collapsing into each other's arms as you prop one another up through the climatic stages of the game can be a sexual experience in itself.

Unfortunately, squash is usually not so much about being nice to one another as about being nasty. So do be careful. That sweet young thing, who looks ever so harmless, and holds the racket with both of her tiny

hands, and who can't remember (so she says) how to serve and who asks you to 'be gentle with her', may not turn out to be all that harmless when you get down to business. And you may soon discover that the business you thought you were getting down to is not quite what she has in mind.

Not that the truth always dawns all that quickly: it is all too easy to let yourself be led on by her apparent innocence for quite some time until the grim reality suddenly hits you when she says sweetly: 'Now, have I got the score clear? It's eight points to me, and none to you, and I'm still serving, right? You know, I think I'm really beginning to enjoy this game.'

○ RULES OF SQUASH ○ RACKETS

No racket is like any other racket

The newer the racket, the greater the chances of it getting broken

Somewhere there's a racket that's just right for each one of us – but no one ever finds it

You happiest moments with your new racket will be those before you discover that you can't play any better with it than you could with your old one

Banging your racket against the wall doesn't usually make you play any better

You are more likely to blame your racket than yourself

Keeping a racket on the back window ledge of your car is no indication that you can play squash

9 The After Game

'I've a grand memory for forgetting'

Robert Louis Stevenson, Kidnapped

Even if the points tally is against you when you stagger off court after a game, the Survival Squasher can always draw some consolation from the fact that things are by no means over yet. There is still the 'after-game' to come. And this is invariably where the accomplished Survival Squasher really comes into his own.

The 'after-game' is essentially a continuation of the game by other means – psychological this time rather than physical – when both players try to square accounts about what actually happened out there on the court. Skilfully played, it can enable the Survival Squasher to turn the tables on an opponent who *thought* the match was his.

So, whatever you do, don't let him try to sneak out of the after-game. Watch out for those types who try to slide off after the match – taking a quick shower, chalking up the result (if he won) and then skipping off home before you can offer to buy him a pint.

The Survival Squasher should on no account allow this to happen. However broken you feel, this is your chance. Your opponent may have demolished you on court; but now you can go to work on him. What you may have failed to do in the pit, you can now do at the bar (while numbing those aches and pains into the bargain).

The first part of the after-game usually consists of a joint analysis of the match, trying to see what went right and what went wrong (and for whom). It's important here not to let the facts and figures of the encounter put you off your stroke – even if it was 9-0, 9-0, 9-0 to him, and you were suffering from premature rigor mortis by the end.

This sort of detail should be easy enough to blur and forget once a good Survival Squasher gets his elbows on the bar. Invariably, in fact, the Survival Squasher tends to find that his whole view of the game changes considerably in retrospect – usually for the better. Thus, even after what appeared to be an abject defeat, try to make sure that your tone is upbeat and jovial (as soon as you can summon up the energy). In fact, you can confide heartily to your opponent, you are very much looking forward to another encounter – but *next time* when you are *fully fit* (which may, of course, not be for some while).

Anyone listening (and try to make sure that as many people as possible *are*) might be forgiven for thinking that you thoroughly enjoyed yourself down there – even, possibly, that *you* were the one who won. If you can afford it, this impression can often be encouraged by buying drinks all round in apparent celebration. (Provided you made a point of playing on your usual ropey old back court without the gallery, there should be no witnesses around to correct this impression.)

Your opponent, of course, may seek to put the record straight (as he sees it). But if he's the dedicated sort who's better on court than he is at the bar, he probably won't be much of a match for you at dispensing the bonhomie. In fact, his growing irritation may serve only to create an impression that he's a bit miffed at how the game actually went.

If, however, he does try to take you up on any of your observations, it's best to avoid getting into a squabble over details, and to simply play down the significance of the whole encounter: 'Well, I felt that was a good workout for both of us. Shouldn't be too long now before I'm really on form.'

Another trick is to make sure that *you* do most of the talking about *his* game. (Surprisingly, people don't mind this – they often prefer to talk about their own game.)

'That corkscrew serve of yours is really devasting, Joe. You certainly caught me out with that a few times. But it could do so much more damage, you know, if you could disguise it better and perhaps even put a little backspin on it'.

'I liked those flicks of yours down the line out of the backhand corner. Once you manage to get your racket right down to them – parallel to the floor – they're going to be real winners.'

It's at this point that the Survival Squasher – now that he's had a bit of a

breather – can really *show* that he's beginning to get back into his old form again. This is where he slides off his barstool (steadying himself on the bar if necessary) and offers his opponent – and everyone else – a demonstration of exactly what he means by 'getting down to those low balls', as he plays a few shadow strokes in slow motion. (The Survival Squasher's shots often come off a lot better when he doesn't have a ball to chase.) There is no harm in clarifying your demonstration by drawing a few diagrams in beer on the bar.

Of course it may eventually dawn on the assembled company that you actually *lost.* (Your opponent, for instance, may be ill-mannered enough to blurt this out.) But, if this happens, you should still be able to salvage the situation – provided that your opponent isn't rude enough to blurt out the score as well. The thing to do is to portray the match as a rather close encounter – while at the same time giving him every credit for his victory:

'That was a tough one, Joe. But there's no question that you deserved it. Watch out next time, though, I'll be wanting my revenge.' (You are, in fact, in the process of taking it at this precise moment.)

Don't, however, make this sound like too much of a challenge. He may then retort 'That'll be the day', and start getting aggressive about it. If he does start getting prickly the best thing is to massage his ego (while continuing to patronise him at the same time):

'You really are getting better all the time, Joe. With a little more work, I'm almost sure you could get into the team. I'll have a word with the skipper if you like.'

In fact, the more you build *him* up, the more you are building yourself up – especially as, by all accounts (yours, at any rate), it was *such a close thing.* It might so easily have been a different story, but you 'just couldn't get your eye in'. You just 'weren't flowing'; couldn't 'get your rhythm going'; 'kept making errors' (of the *unforced* variety, of course – you don't want to give him the credit).

Now you will find occasions when your opponent will persist in trying to shed a somewhat different light on the game – especially if *he* won: after all, it's usually the winner's privilege to give the loser a few tips about the game. Fortunately, however, winners are usually more modest than losers and somewhat inclined to rest on their laurels.

So, if you keep at it, it should be possible to ensure that *your* version of what happened predominates over *his* – whatever the score may suggest.

Incidentally, if the score should happen to be a bit lop-sided, don't let him make too much of it: 'I never feel the scoreline tells the whole story, do you Joe?'

Another approach is to let your opponent do your talking for you. This requires you to adopt a more humble downcast attitude, playing on his sympathies, and leading him on with remarks like: 'You're much too fit for me, I'm afraid.' This may persuade him, if he's a decent sort of chap, to say: 'Nonsense. You had me worried a lot of the time. I didn't feel I was really safe until we walked out of that door.' (There may be no small measure of truth in this, given the way you were flailing about with your racket.)

Now all this does rather tend to presuppose that you lost. It is entirely possible – probable even – that you won (however dubiously), dedicated Survival Squasher that you are. In this instance, it might be your opponent who is seeking his revenge. Make sure, though, that he doesn't get it: a Survival Squasher may not triumph on-court every time but he never loses the after-game.

○ RULES OF SQUASH ○ BOOKING A COURT

The courts will all be booked at the time when you want to play

The fact that you have booked a court does not mean that someone else has not booked the same court

There's always one court no one wants to play on. That will be the only one left

Someone will be playing on the wrong court

The people before you on court won't finish their match on time

Nor will you

However long you book the court for will be *too* long

10 Après-Squash

'British manhood . . . fearing nothing but closing time'

Arthur M. Binstead

As with the after-game, après-squash is an activity where the accomplished Survival Squasher should prove more than a match for most challengers. In fact, many Survival Squashers turn out to be 'naturals' at après-squash. This is, perhaps, not so surprising. For, if the game is all about pain and suffering, après-squash is more about self-indulgence and thus rather more in the Survival Squasher's line.

It works the other way too: you invariably find that the aggressive health-obsessed types who shine on court are not nearly such good performers *after* the match. It's not just that they lack the Survival Squasher's talent for making whoopee. Many of them simply don't have the stamina to stay the course.

The fact is that après-squash can be pretty hard on the system. And it's not everyone who can stand up to a full night's 'squash' – twenty minutes on court, a bout of energetic horseplay in the locker-room (flicking the wet towels around), followed by seven pints of Guinness.

The Survival Squasher, however, does know how to pace himself and how to hang in there for the duration. Some even manage to put in their '500 skips after the game' just to make it clear to their opponents that there's more to the game than just the game.

This is what the 'real' Squashers often fail to appreciate. They channel all their energy and aggression into the match and as a result they burn themselves out too early. The Survival Squasher, in contrast, sees to it that he 'peaks' at the bar, showing who really has a tiger in his tank. Those dedicated wall-bashers may be able to play *to* the gallery. But when it comes to playing *from* the gallery – pint-in-hand, commentating on the antics of others – they're just not in the same league as the Survival Squasher.

As already indicated, however, in order to make the most of his talents the Survival Squasher needs to 'play' at the right sort of club. So avoid the sort of place that doesn't permit smoking and hasn't got itself licensed to serve alcohol. Squash should be a high-risk game, both on and off the court, with as much chance of pegging out from cirrhosis of the liver as from a heart attack during a game. This means playing at the sort of club where there are at least some people who enjoy a good time, a club that's strong on the social side.

After all, isn't this one of the reasons why people play – to meet other people? There's nothing to be ashamed of, therefore, if most of the dates in the Survival Squasher's diary are not matches, but social events; if he looks forward more to the Saturday night disco, or to the punch-and-pâté party, or to the Roaring Twenties evening than he does to his next league match; if even a quiet evening with just a pint of the club's fizzy keg beer and some potato salad on a paper plate seems preferable to eating your words on court.

You can even make the game a bit of a social occasion. This is why

many male Survival Squashers choose to play in the lower leagues: the competition is less fierce, and you do tend to meet more members of the opposite sex. Squash clubs, of course, can be a very good place for clandestine meetings with someone other than your regular partner. (Just one more reason for playing on that dimly lit back court without the gallery.)

There's certainly no reason to feel ashamed if, from time to time, you give priority to your prurient interests. On the contrary. In any clashes with 'real' squashers, it's a chance to show that this is another department where you are well ahead of them, and that there is more than one meaning to the phrase 'a good length'.

To succeed in this sort of way, you often will have to call on the help of other Survival Squashers. It's usually easy enough to enlist a partner as a 'stooge', who can ask you loudly at the appropriate moment, in the vicinity of one of your rivals: 'Who was up till 3 o'clock last night, then? And who with, eh?

Unlike real squashers, Survival Squashers do realise that squash is a *team* game. This also goes for other key figures around the club, like the barmaid, who can often do a good deal for a male Survival Squasher's reputation if he gets on the right side of her. You can do this by helping her behind the bar, learning how to fix the microwave and so on.

Your aim here is to allow your opponents to infer that there may be more between you and Mabel than meets the eye, and that the reason for your poor performance on court may be that you were saving your energy for something else. Even an apparently harmless remark like: 'When are we shutting tonight, Mabel?' can be enough to imply that there are some parts of you which your opponent's game has not managed to reach. This impression can only be enhanced if Mabel can be trained to lovingly make up your own 'special brew' for you in your own special mug after the game.

As well as Mabel, its also important to keep on good terms with your club mates – especially the survival sort. If you've picked the right sort of club there should be no shortage of people who prefer to watch telly at the club rather than doing so at home. It's true that some of these people can be a bit of a pain – the bar bore and the club wally – but they're worth cultivating nonetheless. If you do your best to boost their morale ('I bet you were pretty good in your day'), they'll do their best to reward you – treating you with a certain respect and perhaps giving you a fearsome nickname like Godzilla.

As well as getting to know the lousy players, or the lousy non-players, you should also make a point of rubbing shoulders and being seen to rub shoulders with the star players. They, too, can be susceptible to flattery; and your admiration for them will tend to lead them to believe that you must know a bit about the game. Make sure, of course, that you never actually *play* these people; that way they won't feel aggressive towards you or, for that matter, contemptuous; and they may even not take it amiss if you take them aside now and again to give them a word of advice.

It's important to be on good terms with all the key figures of the club – the President, his wife, the team captain, the club secretary and the coach. (It can also be worthwhile to be on apparently familiar terms with prominent squash figures who aren't actually members of your club. Thus, you can always refer to Barrington as 'Jonah', and Jahan as 'Hiddy'.)

The best way to get on close terms with the club hierarchy is to become one of the club busybodies. True, this can mean having to give up a good deal of your time; but it will at least provide you with a good excuse for not going on court too often, and it will ensure that you become identified with the people at the club who matter.

There's no shortage of chores at any club that can keep you occupied in this way. Even performing some of the more menial tasks can establish you as a vital figure – volunteering for bar duty, keeping the reservation book, developing an expertise for fixing the telly . . . . But you can also go in for more ambitious projects: organising children's coaching weeks; getting a club T-shirt made up; arranging squash video evenings, Old Tyme Music Hall nights or whist drives; inviting an SRA technical specialist to advise on court maintenance; getting top players along to play exhibitions; arranging bus trips to the British Open. Always make it clear, of course, that you are doing all this *for them*, your club mates – whether you are campaigning to get a new court constructed or to get real ale laid on.

Surprisingly enough, it's often this sort of off-court activity, rather than your prowess *on*-court, which can even get you onto such key bodies as the Seeding and Selection Committee. You can thus find yourself in a position to make or break the club stars, some of whom will be desperate to curry favour with you (especially if they're in danger of being relegated to the 'B' team). Even doing the league chart can ensure that everyone will be anxious to keep in with you in the hope that you will exercise your discretion in their favour in deciding who goes up and who goes down.

As we've indicated, however, this sort of activity can be extremely time-consuming. Thus, you may prefer to establish yourself simply by becoming a master (or mistress) of the arts of 'squash talk'. This means that instead of occupying yourself helping behind the bar or working out the league chart, you spend your time sitting side-saddle on the window ledge of the show court, as a self-appointed 'marker' of other people's games, calling out 'Time' or 'Footfault' at appropriate moments. You'll also undoubtedly have a certain amount of advice to offer, calling down: 'Stretch for it', 'More air, John'; 'Corkscrew lob, John', 'Trickle boast, now, John'. Any boasting you do, of course, will invariably tend to be *off* the court:

'Done too much coaching in my time to be much of a match player any more. Still, we've got to make way for the youngsters sometime.'

'Did take a couple of points off Hashim Khan once, but certainly couldn't these days.'

To ensure your dominance at squash talk, it's important to be well up with all the more obscure terminology of the game, so that if anyone takes you on in this area, you can come up with the odd conversation-stopper like: 'I wouldn't say cocking his wrist is his problem. More like *ineffective forearm pronation*, if you ask me.'

A good deal of your expertise won't be about the game itself but about facilities and equipment – enabling you to hold forth on everything from squash shoes and string tension to condensation and court construction.

Important as squash talk is, though, you cannot afford to neglect the physical side of après-squash, which also requires a good deal of hard training. You may not always feel as if you are 'raring to go', but you should always *look* as though you are. In fact, you see so many people slumped across the bar after their matches that it's not so hard to cut a good figure and look fit and energetic as you make a point of *not* leaning on the bar.

You should make sure, therefore, that your own training programme is geared very specifically to après-squash. You need a very different kind of fitness to put away those seven pints and to indulge in your off-court letching. And, like all training, it can be hard going at times. But it has to be done. If your opponents can outlast you in the pit, you must be able to outlast them in the sauna. They may play better squash, but you can eat a hotter curry. You may not have the puff for the game, but you've got plenty of wind when it comes to telling shaggy-dog stories and criticising other players.

You may lose more liquid than your opponent during a match, but you can put a lot back in afterwards. He may be better at cocking his wrist, but he'll be no match for you at bending the old elbow. You may at times lose your grip on the game, but you're always game for a grope off-court. You may not be able to rally all day, but you can rave away all night.

In fact, as we noted earlier, the kind of fitness required for après-squash is so different that you often find that the star players just can't cut the mustard off-court. Their legs start to go and they just fade away at the bar or at the disco. And this is not just on those occasions when they're knackered themselves on court beforehand. The fact is that members of

the club team are not usually noted for their performances at club rave-ups – the Christmas disco, New Year's Eve, the club dinner, Roaring Forties nights, key-swapping parties etc.

The reason for this may be that, unlike when they're on-court, off-court the star players can all too easily find themselves in situations they cannot *control*. And it is certainly true that these 'club nites' do tend to get out of hand. People start chucking the bread rolls about, telling vulgar stories, taking their clothes off and playing silly games.

You may find it worthwhile, incidentally, to devote a good deal of your training to mastering just one of these silly games. Thus, when it comes to seeing who can do the most press-ups perched on four bottles of beer, you'll be able to humiliate even the fittest player in the club. Mastery of this sort of skill should enable you to fend off any of the club aces who try to challenge you to a showdown on-court. Usually you need only to issue a veiled threat about a 'return match' afterwards to make him back off. Try:

'See you at our breakdance evening.'
'I hope you're coming to our rugger-buggers night.'

As we've stressed often enough, however, après-squash can take it out of you. And there may be times when you wonder whether it might not be easier to devote yourself to the game itself. One thing is for sure. It's very hard to combine both. That's why many Survival Squashers try to get their playing over and done with early in the season. That way they can hold their place in the league while everyone is still unfit, and then retire gracefully to the social scene. (It's much the same sort of logic that players use when they get knocked out of the tournament: a 'blessing in disguise', they tend to say, 'now I can concentrate on the league.')

Of course, it's never possible to avoid the game entirely. Even the most skilled après-squasher finds himself treading the boards from time to time. But by concentrating on your *off*-court game, you should be able to minimise these occasions and to more than make up for any of your weaknesses on court.

When you come to think of it, this phenomenon may even be the explanation for those unbelievable SRA statistics about *one Briton in twenty* 'playing' squash these days. The SRA probably haven't allowed for all those who have devoted themselves to après-squash; or who just keep a racket in their brief-case and play the occasional verbal game over lunch or on the train to and from work.

As we said at the outset, there's more than one way of playing the game.